CATS & DOGS

by Francine Hughes

SCHOLASTIC INC.
New York Toronto London Auckland Sydney
Mexico City New Delhi Hong Kong
Buenos Aires

D1472389

Copyright ™ & © 2001 Warner Bros.
All rights reserved. Published by Scholastic Inc.
SCHOLASTIC and associated logos are trademarks and/or registered trademarks of Scholastic Inc.

ISBN 0-439-22573-6

10 9 8 7 6 5 4 3 2   1 2 3 4 5 6

Design by Louise Bova

Printed in the U.S.A.
First Scholastic printing, June 2001

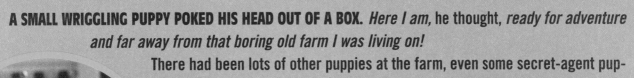

A SMALL WRIGGLING PUPPY POKED HIS HEAD OUT OF A BOX. *Here I am,* he thought, *ready for adventure and far away from that boring old farm I was living on!*

There had been lots of other puppies at the farm, even some secret-agent puppies that had shown up just in time for Mrs. Brody's visit. But out of all the dogs to choose from, Professor Brody's wife had picked this little foxhound.

Now Mrs. Brody set the box on the kitchen floor. "Scott," she called to her eleven-year-old son. "I've got a surprise for you."

Scott looked up from his homework just as the excited puppy jumped out of the box. But then Scott turned his back, not interested at all.

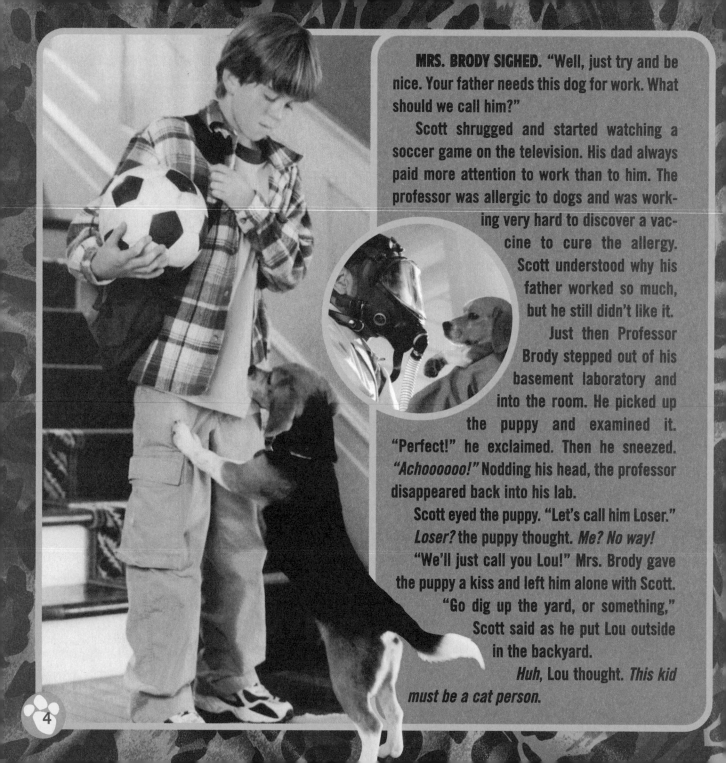

MRS. BRODY SIGHED. "Well, just try and be nice. Your father needs this dog for work. What should we call him?"

Scott shrugged and started watching a soccer game on the television. His dad always paid more attention to work than to him. The professor was allergic to dogs and was working very hard to discover a vaccine to cure the allergy. Scott understood why his father worked so much, but he still didn't like it.

Just then Professor Brody stepped out of his basement laboratory and into the room. He picked up the puppy and examined it. "Perfect!" he exclaimed. Then he sneezed. *"Achoooooo!"* Nodding his head, the professor disappeared back into his lab.

Scott eyed the puppy. "Let's call him Loser." *Loser?* the puppy thought. *Me? No way!*

"We'll just call you Lou!" Mrs. Brody gave the puppy a kiss and left him alone with Scott.

"Go dig up the yard, or something," Scott said as he put Lou outside in the backyard.

Huh, Lou thought. *This kid must be a cat person.*

LOU WANDERED AROUND THE BACKYARD. When he happened to look up at the sky he saw a bright balloon drifting down toward him. When he looked closer at the balloon, there was a yummy-looking dog biscuit hanging from its string! Lou had always wondered where biscuits came from. *So that's where biscuits are made,* he thought. *In the sky.*

When the balloon landed, Lou edged close to the treat and opened his mouth wide.

"I wouldn't do that," said a voice.

Surprised, Lou froze just in time. Boom! The biscuit exploded.

Lou turned around and found himself looking into the face of a serious Labrador retriever. "Name's Butch," said the dog. "Ready for your assignment?"

LOU WAS VERY EXCITED ABOUT GETTING AN ASSIGNMENT. Finally, he was going to get a real adventure! But at that moment, his tail was also pretty interesting. He started chasing his tail while Butch talked to him. It didn't take long for the older agent to realize that Lou was no agent at all.

Butch gasped in shock. "You're just a normal puppy!" he said to Lou. This was not good. How could Butch, an old-time agent, be expected to work with an amateur? Butch quickly pushed his disappointment aside. "There's no time to replace you," he told Lou. "So here's what's going on."

Butch took Lou into his doghouse, which was filled with computers and special equipment. "Dogs have always been man's best friend," Butch explained. "But cats want to control the planet. They want to steal Professor Brody's vaccination formula and change it to cure cat allergies. Then *they'll* be man's best friend. Your mission is to keep the cats away from the lab."

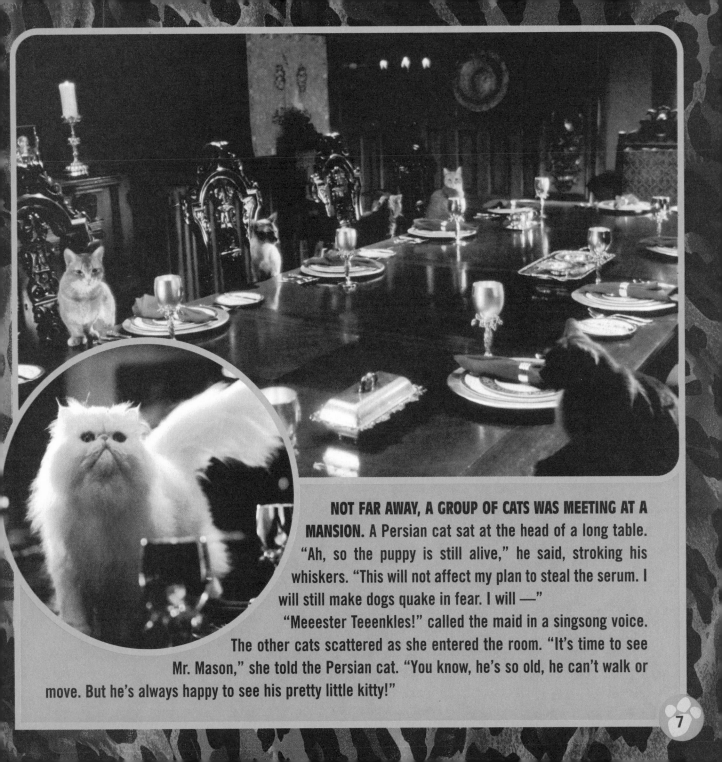

NOT FAR AWAY, A GROUP OF CATS WAS MEETING AT A MANSION. A Persian cat sat at the head of a long table. "Ah, so the puppy is still alive," he said, stroking his whiskers. "This will not affect my plan to steal the serum. I will still make dogs quake in fear. I will —"

"Meeester Teeenkles!" called the maid in a singsong voice. The other cats scattered as she entered the room. "It's time to see Mr. Mason," she told the Persian cat. "You know, he's so old, he can't walk or move. But he's always happy to see his pretty little kitty!"

THAT NIGHT, MR. TINKLES PUT HIS PLAN INTO ACTION. A group of Siamese cats dropped from planes straight onto the Brodys' roof. They were specially trained ninja cats! One by one, they slunk down the chimney and set to work, breaking down the lab door.

Members of Butch's dog team — Sam, Peek, and Ivy — alerted Lou to danger in the house. Lou patrolled each room, but didn't see the cats until he got to the kitchen. Actually, it was Butch who saw them first.

"Kid! Look out behind you!" Butch shouted from outside the window.

A CAT ATTACK! Lou ducked, barely missing sharp claws. One cat stood on its hind legs and held up its paws. *Karate!* thought Lou. *Swat! Slash!* Lou lifted his paws in defense. Right, left, right, left, kick. He fought back bravely while Butch coached him. Garbage flew everywhere as the fighting continued all over the kitchen.

Suddenly, the light flipped on.

"Who's there?" called Mrs. Brody. In a flash, the cats disappeared up the chimney.

The Professor and Mrs. Brody gazed at the mess in the room. "Lou!" Mrs. Brody scolded as she scooped him up and put him outside. "You're lucky you're so cute."

THE NEXT MORNING, MR. TINKLES PUT A NEW PLAN INTO ACTION: He sent his best secret agent to the Brody house, a deadly Russian Blue kitten.

"She's just a poor lost kitty," Mrs. Brody explained as she brought the dainty kitten inside. The kitten purred sweetly, nuzzling Lou. Mrs. Brody left, and the purr turned into a snarl.

"You are in trouble," hissed the cat in a deep, menacing voice. He coughed up a hair ball that contained a ticking bomb inside.

BUTCH RACED INTO THE KITCHEN TO HELP LOU. "Ha!" sneered the cat, coughing up another hair ball. He flung it at the dogs. The ball opened. Knives flew out, hurtling straight at Lou and Butch!

Quickly, Lou dove for cover. Butch jumped onto a tall cabinet. The cabinet swayed, then fell forward. Butch yelped, tumbling to the ground, tangling his paws in the wires on the hairball bomb. The cabinet came to a stop and caught on some drapes. *Creak!* The cabinet tilted dangerously. The drapes were ripping!

"HANG ON, BUTCH!" LOU CRIED. "I'M COMING!"

"Hey, puppy!" called the kitten as he tossed a boomerang. "Fetch!" Lou couldn't help but obey. He ran for the boomerang. *Whoosh!* It lifted him off the ground, whisking him around the room and *smash!* — right into the kitten. Just then, the curtain ripped apart. "Ugh!" groaned Butch, scrambling free as the cabinet crashed to the floor.

TICK, TICK, TICK. ONE SECOND, AND THE BOMB WOULD BLOW. Butch raced to cut the wires. "There!" he cried, snipping them just in time.

"You have not won yet!" cried the kitten, glowering at Lou and Butch.

The lab door slammed open, pinning the kitten against the wall. "Here, boy!" called Professor Brody, walking into the room. He lifted Lou and held him close. Immediately, his nose turned bright red. "But no sneezing!" he declared. "All I need is a little more work!"

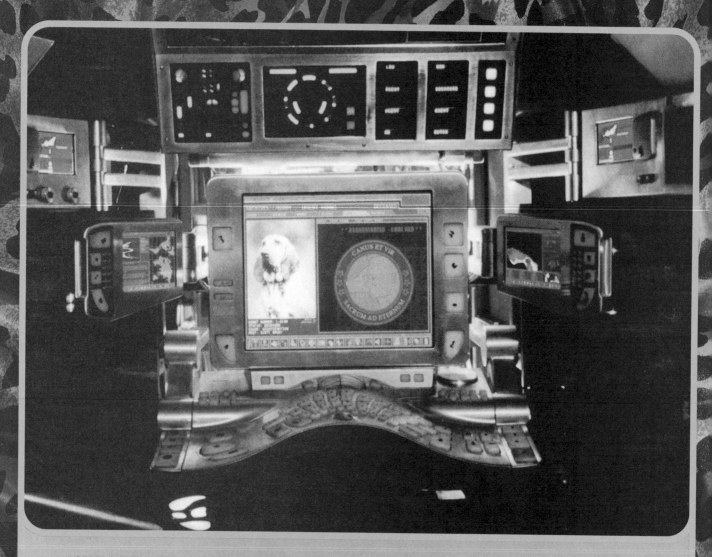

SAM, PEEK, AND IVY DELIVERED THE KITTEN TO HEADQUARTERS, then helped clean up the Brody house before any of the family came home. Later, Butch led Lou to the doghouse to get the report. "Experts have examined the cat," the head collie told them over the monitor screen, "and found this chewed-up note."

She held up a crumpled piece of paper. "'This is the address where we will enact my fiendish plan,'" Lou read. On one corner, he noticed there was a picture of a Christmas tree.

A CHRISTMAS TREE, Lou repeated to himself as he left the doghouse. *What could it mean?*

Then Lou saw Scott kicking a soccer ball in the backyard all by himself. *The boy looks sad,* Lou thought. *He wants to spend more time with his dad, but maybe we can have some fun, too.*

Lou ran up to the ball, then nosed it back to Scott. Scott kicked it back. Lou chased it, barking happily. They laughed and played, and then Scott kicked the ball too hard. It rolled into the house, bouncing right through the open lab door.

"UH-OH!" SAID SCOTT. THEY RACED DOWN THE STEPS AFTER IT, BUT IT WAS TOO LATE. The ball bounced onto a shelf and rolled to the edge! If it fell off it would bounce into a beaker of bubbling orange liquid and a nearby computer that was analyzing the formula.

Lou gasped. Horrified, he knocked the ball away, but it slammed right into a rack full of beakers. The beakers crashed to the ground and all the chemicals mixed together just as Professor Brody came down the stairs.

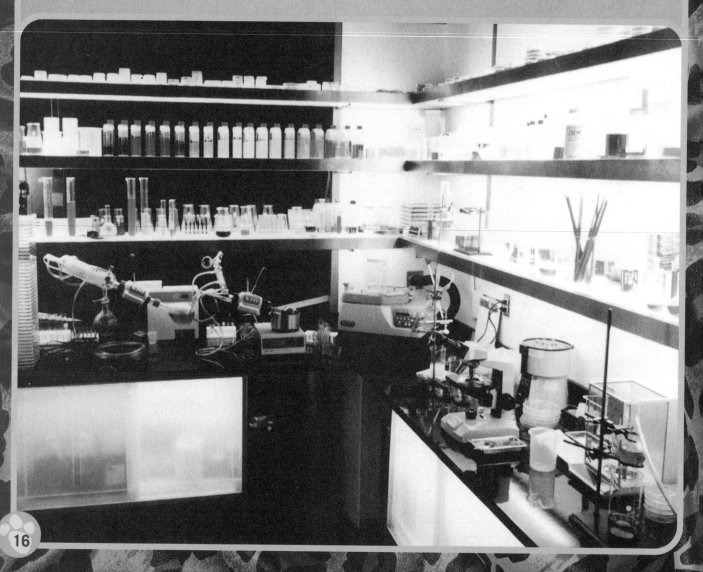

"MY WORK!" the professor shouted, running into the lab. Then he glanced at the computer. "What? Could *this* formula work?"

All of the orange chemicals had turned green. The professor mixed the chemicals into a vaccine, gave himself a shot, then sniffed Lou. Nothing. No red nose. No sneezes. No allergic reaction at all.

"I did it!" shouted the Professor. "We did it!"

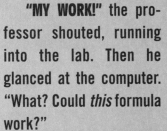

IMMEDIATELY, PROFESSOR BRODY CALLED HIS OFFICE WITH THE NEWS. He'd discovered the cure for dog allergies! Listening in on a secret device, Mr. Tinkles grinned. "Our day has come!" he howled. Quickly, the cats dressed Mr. Mason, then drove him in his limousine to the company Mr. Mason owned: Mason Flocking Inc., a factory where hundreds of trees were sprayed with fake snow.

BACK AT THE BRODY HOUSE, SCOTT WAS OPENING A PACKAGE. "I won free tickets to tonight's soccer game!" he cried. He wasn't expecting his parents to take him. He thought his dad would be working. But that night, they drove to the stadium.

"We must be early," said the professor, opening the window to gaze at the empty parking lot. While the family looked around, a smoking canister flew into the car filling it with sleeping gas. The next thing the Brodys knew, they were prisoners inside the Christmas tree factory!

NOT LONG AFTER, A CALICO CAT STRUTTED CALMLY OVER TO LOU AND BUTCH. He dropped a videotape at their paws. Seconds later, they were watching the tape. Lou gasped. The Brody family was being held hostage in some sort of office!

Then Mr. Tinkles came on screen to deliver his evil message. "You are to bring the formula and all notes regarding Professor Brody's research to the Ninth Street Bridge at dawn. If you refuse, the family will be put to sleep!"

"WE'RE GONNA SAVE THEM, RIGHT?" LOU ASKED BUTCH.

"Kid, we're going to headquarters!" Butch announced, leading Lou to the doghouse. Lou had been wondering where headquarters was. Now Butch pressed a button and seats sprang up from the floor. Butch and Lou fell in.

"A rocket sled!" Lou exclaimed.

Click! Safety straps snapped around them. A canopy lowered over their heads and a hole opened below. The agents dropped like a shot, careening through tubes and tunnels.

When they reached headquarters, Lou jumped out and followed Butch to a large conference room. Dogs from around the world were deciding what to do: Save the family? Or save the formula?

HOURS LATER, THE DOG GOVERNMENT REACHED A DECISION.

The conference had voted to sacrifice the family in order to keep the formula safe.

"Nooo!" screamed Lou as the rocket sled brought them back to the Brody house. "I don't want to lose my family!"

"We have our orders," barked Butch.

But Lou wouldn't listen. As soon as he was alone, he came up with a plan. He dumped the formula in a wagon, and raced to meet the Persian cat at the bridge.

BUTCH FIGURED OUT LOU'S SCHEME AND CAUGHT UP WITH HIM JUST AS THE PUPPY reached the center of the bridge. Suddenly, the bridge shuddered, then rose and split in two. It was a drawbridge! Butch and Lou held on tight to the top of one side, but the wagon hurtled down the other side — straight to Mr. Tinkles.

"Hello, my foolish foes!" the cat laughed. "I'll work on this formula right away. But first, I have one little thing to do. Even though you followed orders, it's time to put the Brodys to sleep!"

LOU RACED HOME. HE HAD TO SAVE HIS FAMILY! Lou studied Mr. Tinkles' videotape again and again, looking for a clue to find where the Brodys were being held prisoners.

Finally, Lou gave up. He let the tape run out, thinking there was no more to see. But suddenly, the screen filled with another scene: Mr. Mason's birthday party, left over from an earlier taping. A banner read, MASON FLOCKING, INC. Lou had always wondered where those fake snow-covered Christmas trees came from. Then he noticed something else.

"Look, Butch!" he cried. "The banner has that same Christmas tree picture on it! I'll bet that's where the Brodys are!"

AT THAT EXACT MOMENT, THE BRODY FAMILY STARED AT MR. TINKLES IN SHOCK. Their kidnapper was a cat? And he could talk? "We've loaded the fake snow with the dog allergy," Mr. Tinkles explained, "and the snow will spread it all over the world!"

Excited, the Persian cat leaped onto the water cooler — water streamed out and splashed a nearby outlet. *Crackle! Sizzle! Pop!* Sparks flew from the outlet, landing on a thick, billowy curtain. *Whoosh!* The curtain went up in flames! Grinning evilly, Mr. Tinkles scampered away, leaving the Brodys alone with the spreading fire.

DOWN ON THE FACTORY FLOOR, MR. TINKLES CALLED TOGETHER HIS SPECIAL ARMY: MICE! "You will all be covered with dog allergy and hidden in snow, and you will carry this snow through the sewers to infect humans everywhere!" he ordered.

A giant sewer hatch opened wide. But suddenly, huge cans rolled across the floor. Butch and Lou jumped out of two of them. *Slam!* They flung the sewer hatch closed.

"AHHHH!" **A WOMAN'S FRIGHTENED SCREAMS ECHOED THROUGHOUT THE FACTORY.** *Mrs. Brody!* Lou thought as he looked up at the fiery office. *My family is up there!* He had to get them. But what about the cats and the mice?

"I'm here," Ivy announced. She held a giant water hose in her paws. "And it's bathtime!" The water rushed out, pouring over the helpless army.

IN A FLASH, LOU DASHED TO THE OFFICE. "LOU!" CRIED SCOTT. "YOU'RE GOING TO SAVE US!"
The little puppy untied the Brodys, then led everyone out of the smoky room, onto a catwalk high above the factory floor. There was a fire exit up ahead. Escape!
But suddenly, a tall crane swung its hook onto the catwalk, blocking their flight. "Ha!" laughed Mr. Tinkles, from behind the controls.

LOU SPUN AROUND AND POINTED TO A GIANT FAN WITH SHARP, SPINNING BLADES. There was another way out!

"We can't go through there!" Mrs. Brody cried.

"We can if we turn it off," said the professor.

Lou rolled a snowman's head over to Scott. Scott nodded, then kicked the head like a soccer ball. It sailed straight through the blades, hitting the switch on the other side. The fan whirred to a stop.

IN A FLASH, LOU HERDED THE FAMILY AND MR. MASON THROUGH THE FAN, where a door led them to safety. "You haven't won yet!" Mr. Tinkles cried, sending the crane into the catwalk.

Thinking fast, Lou turned on the switch again. The blades spun, sucking the crane and Mr. Tinkles into the fan. But the catwalk was collapsing!

Lou fell all the way down to the ground and crashed onto the floor.

"LOU!" CRIED BUTCH. He lifted the puppy and brought him outside to where the Brodys were waiting. Scott gazed at his unmoving friend. "Lou?" he said, tears rolling down his cheeks.

Lou blinked, then opened his eyes. "You're alive!" Scott shouted happily. "I am, too!" Mr. Tinkles cried, behind them. "I've got nine lives! So watch out."

All at once, a hand grabbed the cat, and held him fast. It was Mr. Mason! "Bad kitty!" he said.

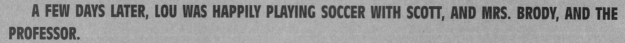

A FEW DAYS LATER, LOU WAS HAPPILY PLAYING SOCCER WITH SCOTT, AND MRS. BRODY, AND THE PROFESSOR.

Professor Brody hugged Scott, proud of his son and glad to be spending time with him. Everything had worked out just fine.

From across the yard, Butch wagged his tail at Lou. The puppy might not have been a *professional* secret agent, but he turned out to be a terrific one, after all.

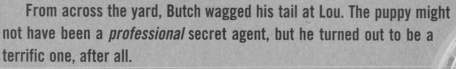

Meanwhile, on the other side of town, Mr. Tinkles was plotting his next evil scheme.